For Denise, who
understands our crew!
— A.D.

For Ame.
— S.M.

"Okay..."

BLARP!

Library of Congress Cataloging-in-Publication Data available
ISBN 978-1-338-11388-4 • 10 9 8 7 6 5 4 3 2 1 •
19 20 21 22 23 • Printed in China 38 • First edition, February 2019
The text type was set in Chelsea Market and
Adrianna Condensed.
Book design by Jess Tice-Gilbert

ACTION!

MISUNDERSTOOD SHARK
FRIENDS DON'T
EAT FRIENDS!

Written by Ame Dyckman

Illustrated by Scott Magoon

Orchard Books
New York
An Imprint of Scholastic Inc.

"We all know you
ate me, Shark!"

"IF I ate you...
where's your proof?"

“Hang on.
I don’t feel so good.”

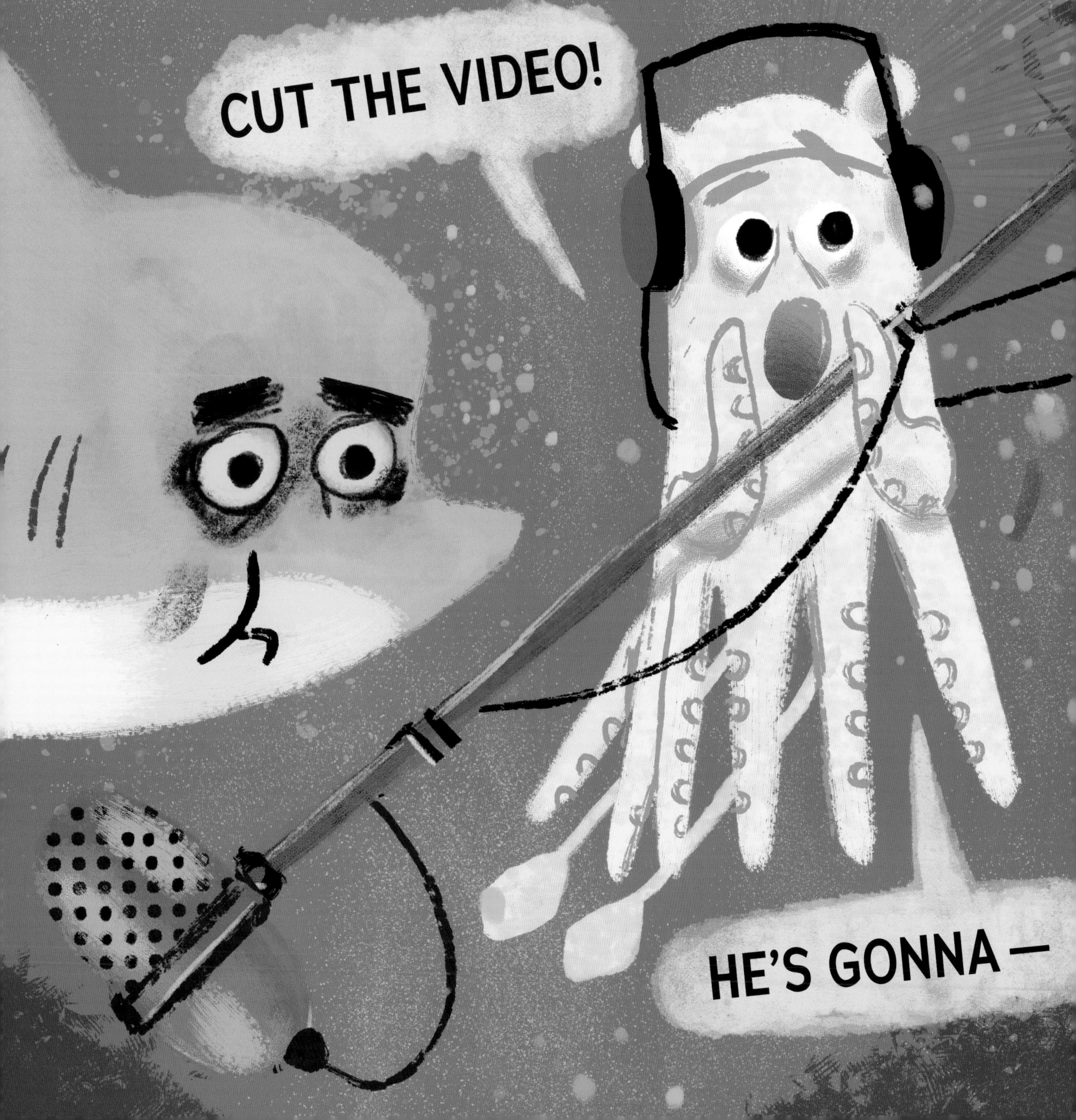

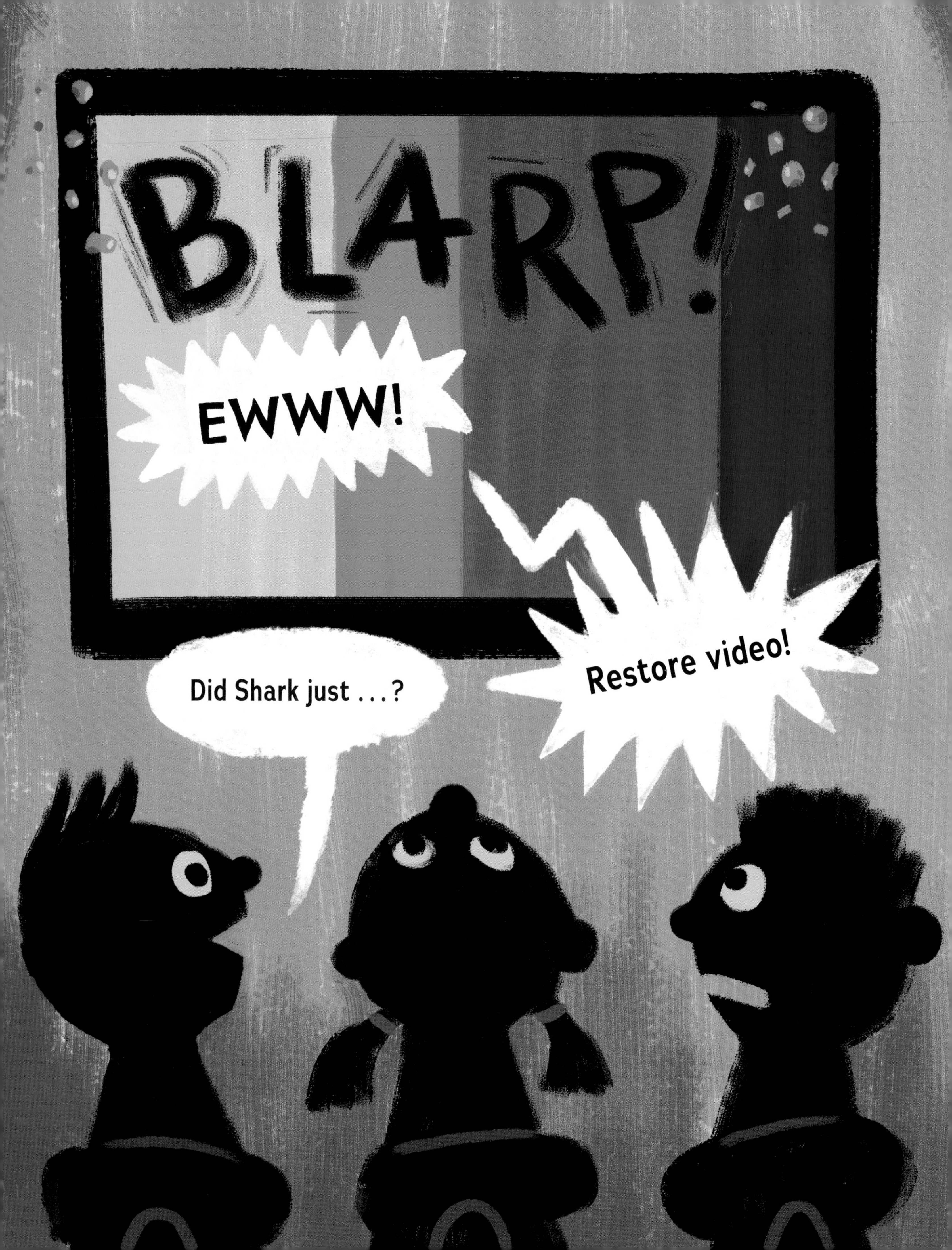
BLARP!
EWWW!
Did Shark just . . . ?
Restore video!

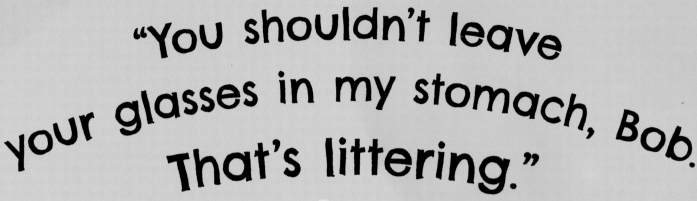

"FRIENDS DON'T EAT FRIENDS!"
"Well . . . FRIENDS DON'T MAKE FRIENDS FEEL BAD ABOUT IT!"

"I do, too!
His name's . . .
Sticky—"

"And he's my
REAL friend—"

"And HE'D never hurt
my feelings like
YOU did!"

"I hurt YOUR
feelings?
BUT YOU ATE ME!"

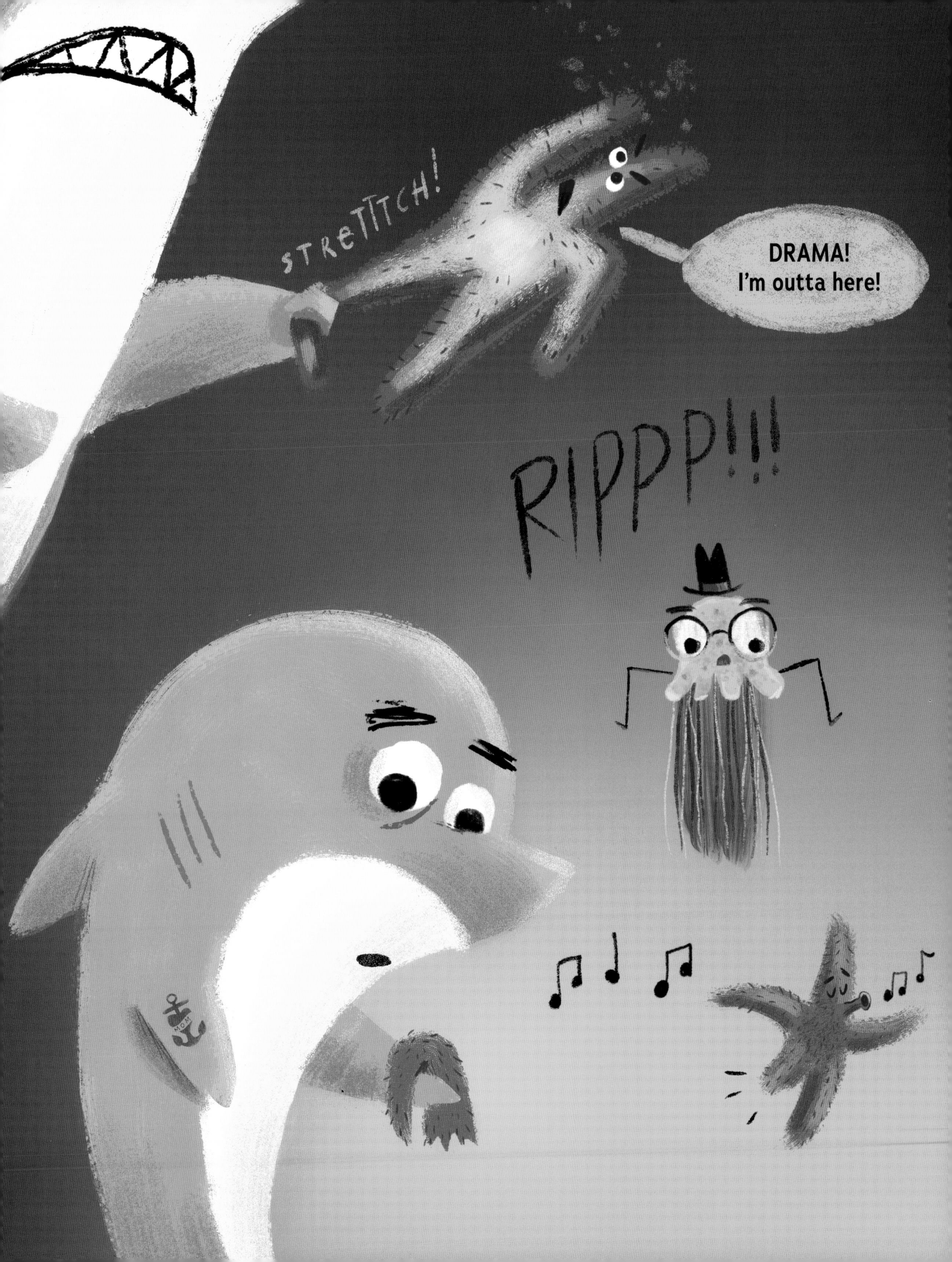
STRETTTCH!
DRAMA!
I'm outta here!
RIPPP!!!

"Okay, I ate you. I'm sorry and I'll try not to eat you again 'cause…"

"You taste gross."

"SHARRRK!"

"I mean..."

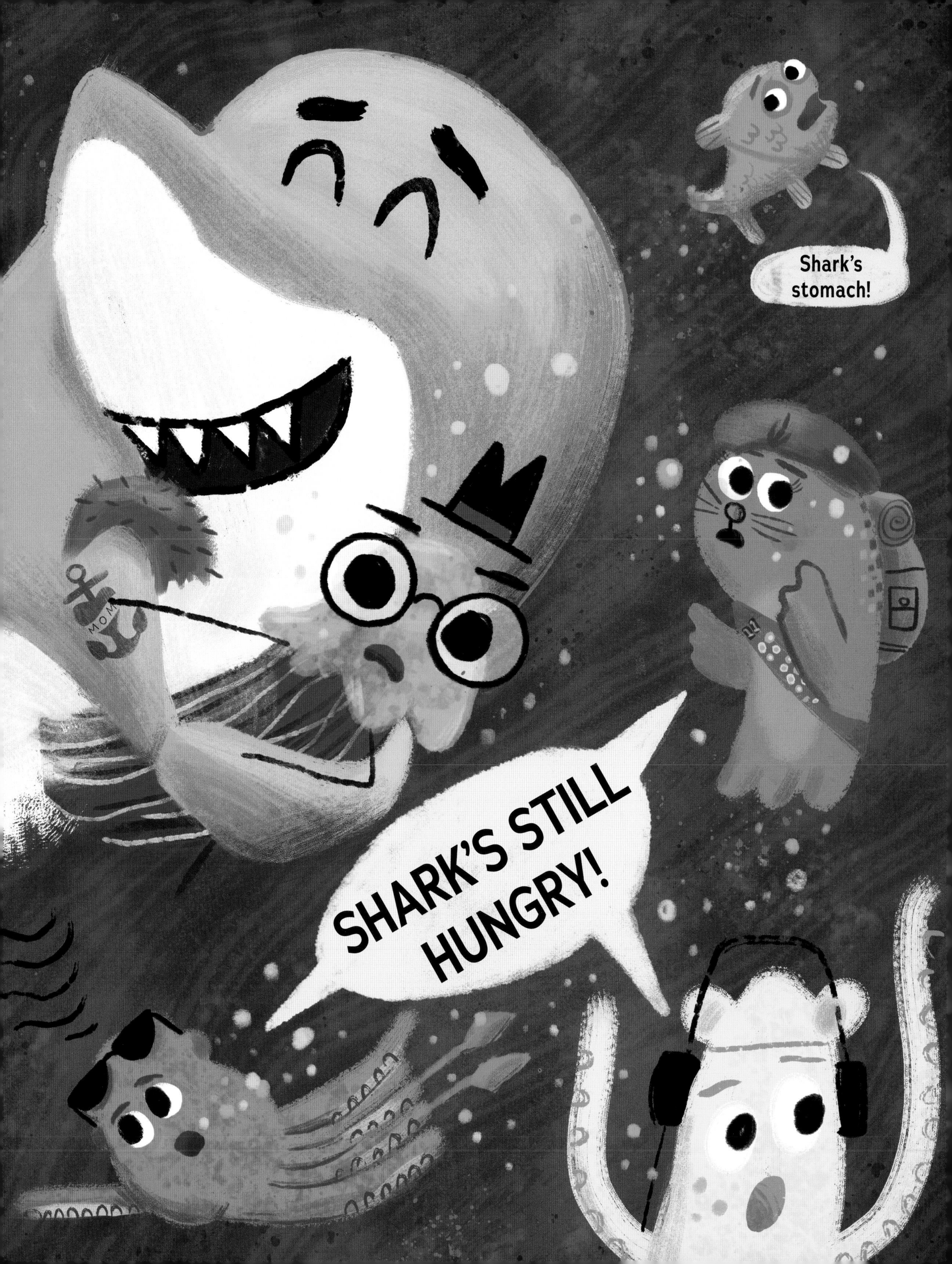
Shark's
stomach!
SHARK'S STILL
HUNGRY!

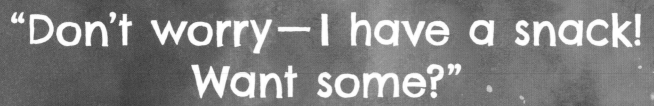